THE JERSEY

TEAM PLAYER

Adapted by Paul Mantell
Based on the series created by Gordon Korman

New York

CONTENTS

CHAPTER ONE

GO, TEAM!

"Red sixty-two! Red sixty-two!" Nick Lighter shouted. The other three members of the Monday Night Football Club huddled around him. "Okay, team, put your hands in here!"

Elliott's hand shot in first—on the bottom of the hand pile, as always. The smallest of the group, Elliott was exactly five feet tall. Like the rest of the Monday Night Football Club, Elliott loved all sports. Skateboarding and rock climbing were his favorites, and he was a computer whiz on top of it.

Coleman's big, strong hand came down on top of Elliott's. Coleman—or "'Slaw," as they all called him—was tall and built like a linebacker. He was all muscle—including his head, Nick liked to joke—which was okay, because Coleman was practically a genius. He had gotten only one B in his entire life, and that was because he'd ticked off the teacher by cracking too many jokes.

Nick waited for his cousin Morgan to put her hand in before he stuck his own on top. But Morgan was waiting on Nick. Morgan was the newest member of the Monday Night Football Club. She and her mom, Nick's aunt April, had moved to town from Chicago a few months before. So who did she think she was? Just because she was smart, popular, pretty, and a great athlete, and knew more about sports than even he did, that didn't make her the leader. That was Nick's job.

Nick's hand was *always* on the top of the pile. He was the one who'd founded the MNFC and gotten the others to join. Morgan didn't seem to understand that *he* was the boss, the top dog, the head honcho. As far as Morgan was concerned, they were all equally in charge. Nick decided that Morgan had a lot to learn.

Nick just had to show her who was in charge. He held back his hand, waiting, and Morgan held hers back, too. "Put your hand in!" he demanded.

"You first." She stared back at him with narrowed eyes, daring him to blink first.

"Come on, you guys!" Elliott urged. "We're wasting time!"

"Yeah," 'Slaw agreed. He and Elliott always agreed. They had been best buddies since they were two, and Nick couldn't think of one time they'd argued.

"Hey, the enemy awaits!" 'Slaw whispered, pointing toward the street.

The enemy. Nick had forgotten about the dreaded trash can ninjas. There they were, lined up on the curb in battle formation. The simple act of taking in the trash cans was about to become a MNFC main event. Glaring angrily at Morgan, Nick stuck his hand on the pile, letting go of their little competition for now. Morgan, smirking in triumph, laid her hand on top of his.

Furious, Nick ignored her and turned his attention to the task at hand: leading his elite team of MNFC samurai ninja warriors into battle.

"Everybody ready?" he asked.

"Ready!" they all shouted.

"Okay. Break!" Hands flew upward. There was a great shout, and together they flew into battle.

Morgan snuck quickly down to the edge of the house. There, she found her way blocked by a menacing bicycle. Letting out a bloodcurdling scream, she grabbed the bike by the handlebars—its weak spot. In the same motion, she faked a head butt, then threw the evil bike over her head. "Hah!" she cried, spinning to face any trash cans foolish enough to attempt an attack.

Nick nodded approvingly. "Well done!" he shouted. "You are learning, young one." He bowed, his palms together, saluting her as a master salutes his pupil.

Morgan ignored him, slinking behind

a tree, getting ready for her next ambush.

Meanwhile, Elliott had slithered across the lawn on his elbows and knees, his eyes darting left and right. He was waiting until the enemies' guard was down. Then, the littlest ninja would spring into action. For now, Elliott waited in perfect stillness.

At the same time, Coleman crept from one tree to another, preparing for the final attack. His hands flew in all directions, wielding invisible ninja stars.

"Kee-yah!" Nick screeched as he elbowed aside a branch and took cover behind the garden fence. From there, he watched the street, waiting for the right moment to send his warriors into action. A car went slowly by, blissfully unaware of the earth-shaking battle taking place nearby.

And then . . .

GO, TEAM!

"Go! Go! Go! Go! Go!" Nick shouted, leaping toward the enemy with blinding speed. Coleman jumped simultaneously, and the attack was on.

"Freeze! You're all nothing but trash!" Elliott yelled, popping up and running at the line of fearsome trash cans.

Suddenly, Nick was there, running up bravely and grabbing one of them by its green plastic ears. He hoisted the can up, throwing it high into the air. The others followed his lead.

As the trash cans descended one by one, Coleman drop-kicked them over a bush to Elliott. Lying on his back with his feet in the air, Elliott kicked the trash cans over to Morgan, who caught them and stacked them into a neat pile, nesting one inside the other, so that they were unable to escape.

The MNFC warriors ran up to high-five each other, yelling in triumph and doing their victory dance. They exchanged the patented MNFC handshake: interlocking their fingers, pointing at each other, then snapping.

Then, right in the middle of their celebration, they saw it, and stopped in their tracks. A lone, forgotten trash can ninja, standing in defiance . . . unbowed, unbeaten.

Nick cracked his knuckles, his expression darkening. "Thought you could get away, huh?" he said to the trash can.

"Let's move in," Elliott suggested.

They advanced together; an unbreakable unit. With a mighty kick, Coleman knocked the trash can into submission. Then the others lined up and group-kicked it into the air. It landed perfectly, nesting in the pile of its defeated trash can brothers.

"It's good!" Nick shouted, holding up his hands to signal a field goal. 'Slaw loaded the prisoners onto the trash can cart, for easy towing back to the Lighters' garage.

It was only after the four friends had washed their hands at the outdoor tap that a grim thought dawned on Nick, and at the same time, on Morgan.

"Homework?" she said, reading his expression.

Nick nodded sadly. There was no avoiding it any longer.

"Ugh!!" Elliott said with a grimace. "History. The dreaded 'group project.'"

"Don't worry about it," Nick assured the others with a smug smile. "I've got millions of ideas."

"Hey, speaking of history," 'Slaw said quickly, "I'm outta here. Not my class. Not my group project. Not my homework."

Morgan put a hand on his shoulder. "Come on, 'Slaw," she pleaded in her sweetest voice. "Help us out. You're so good at this stuff."

It was true, Nick thought. 'Slaw was good at history. He was good at *every* subject. But this was Nick's group, and he knew it was up to *him* to take charge. "Trust me," he assured Elliott and Morgan. "We don't need help." He tapped his head with his index finger and smiled, as if to say, "All the answers are in here."

"What've you got?" 'Slaw asked, always tempted by a challenge.

"What've we got?" Elliott repeated, then heaved a bored sigh. Elliott hated history. "Assignment: Come up with an ad campaign for the Declaration of Independence."

'Slaw's eyes widened. He held up his hands and wiggled his fingers. "Ooo, that makes me all tingly," he said exaggeratedly. "Okay, I'm in."

"Yesss!" Morgan said, giving Coleman the MNFC handshake as they went inside.

Nick stared after them, scowling. What did Morgan think she was doing? They didn't need Coleman. Hadn't he just said so? He followed the others inside, getting more and more annoyed with every passing minute.

CHAPTER TWO

WHO'S THE BOSS?

"How about this: 'Read my lips: no taxation!'" Morgan looked at the rest of them expectantly.

"No, no, no, that one won't work either!" Nick said, tugging at his hair in frustration.

Morgan slammed her notebook shut. "Nick, that's the twelfth idea of mine you've rejected! Not to mention Elliott's and 'Slaw's ideas. What was wrong with *them*?"

Outside, it was already getting dark. They'd been at it for over an hour now, and they'd gotten absolutely nowhere. If only Morgan weren't there, Nick told himself. Elliott and 'Slaw would have gone along with one of his ideas long ago. But Morgan had found something wrong with every one of them, and Nick's two Benedict Arnold friends had agreed with her.

The den was strewn with the results of their efforts so far, all false starts. The floor was littered with markers, stencils, construction paper, and poster board. Right in the middle of the mess sat Coleman and Elliott, looking lost and forlorn.

Finally, Elliott got up and went to the computer, logging on to the Internet. They all sat or stood in silence, listening to the sound of the modem connecting to the server . . . the beeps . . . the static . . .

Nick was fuming. What right did any of them have to be annoyed at him? he thought. Just because he didn't like any of their lame ideas? Well, they *were* lame, and he wasn't going to lie about it, or accept a bad idea, when *he* had plenty of good ones.

Elliott swiveled around in the desk chair, his eyes lit up by an idea for a lead. "Yes! I've got it! Daughters of the American Revolution dot org, we salute you!" he said excitedly. The others looked at him as if he were a Martian. "What? They're cool!" Elliott said defensively.

"Elliott, focus!" Nick ordered, grasping his friend by the shoulders. "No more geeky ideas! This poster has to make a statement!" Nick straightened up and began pacing the room, back and forth, back and forth. "We need a *cool* slogan," he told the others.

Elliott and Coleman stole a glance at each other and shrugged, then looked back at Nick expectantly.

"We're waiting on your 'millions of ideas,'" Morgan said sarcastically.

Nick snorted. What was the matter with them? Didn't they trust him? Wasn't he always the "idea man"?

"Here's one," he offered. "'Fight for Liberty, or Work for a Guy Named George.'" He put his hands out toward them, palms upward, waiting for their response.

They just continued staring at him blankly.

"You know," Nick explained, exasperated. "The King? *George.* Get it?"

'Slaw shook his head. "That," he said, "is pathetic."

"Can't disagree there," Elliott said,

raising his eyebrows.

"Okay," Morgan said, a smile coming over her face. "How about a picture of a Revolutionary War soldier, with the slogan 'Fight for Your Right to Party'?" She glanced around for approval from the others. Nick watched as Elliott and 'Slaw started grinning and nodding like a couple of idiots.

"Contemporary, yet playful," Elliott said.

"I like it," Coleman said approvingly.

Nick gritted his teeth. He knew he had to nip this in the bud. "By 'playful,' do you mean 'ridiculous'?" he asked Elliott.

That drew annoyed looks from all the others. "Nick," Morgan complained, "you've been shooting down everybody else's ideas all night. It's called a 'group project,' remember?"

"Oh, yeah?" Nick shouted, blowing his cool. "Well, maybe I need a different group!" Why did Morgan always have to argue with him? Why couldn't she just follow his lead, like everyone else?

Coleman got up, calm but determined. "Look, you guys," he said, edging toward the door. "Why don't you call me when you're ready to use my services?"

Elliott got up, too, and went over to Coleman. "This negative energy is giving me a stomachache," he said, shaking his head. "I'll do the research—at home."

"Hey!" Nick said. "Where are you guys going? This project is worth a third of our grade!"

"Yeah!" Morgan said, obviously alarmed, and for once agreeing with Nick. "Who's going to do the project if you guys go?"

Elliott shrugged, and pointed to the

two of them. "Apparently, whichever one of *you* wins," he said. And with that, he and Coleman were out the door.

Nick wheeled around, ready to yell at Morgan for blowing everything. But she opened fire first.

"Good job, Nick," she said disgustedly. "You ran off Elliott *and* 'Slaw."

"Me?!" Nick was speechless for a moment, his frustration overflowing. "Yeah, like you had nothing to do with it!"

"Oh, please," Morgan said, rolling her eyes. "I hate to break it to you, genius, but your ideas stink!"

"Mine?" Nick gasped, nearly choking with anger. "Oh, and the 'Revolutionary Fashion Show'—that was a real winner! Thanks, but no thanks. I'll do better on my own."

Morgan threw down her markers and

tape, and headed for the door. "Fine!" she yelled. "You can do the whole thing by yourself!"

"Fine! I will!" Nick shot back. "I'll get an A, too," he bragged. "And you'll *all* have to thank me."

Morgan narrowed her eyes, and her jaw tightened. "In your dreams." She stormed out of the den, leaving Nick alone.

Nick stared around the room, taking in the wreckage that an hour of futile group effort had produced. "I'm better off on my own," he told himself. "A guy like me, with a million good ideas, doesn't need a group anyway."

He was feeling better already. No one to argue with him, or put down his ideas . . .

This was going to be a breeze.

CHAPTER THREE

HILARY STEPS IN

Hilary Lighter sat at the kitchen table, reading a book. Not just any book, though; this book was much more than a good read. It was going to totally change her life!

How to Handle 1,000 Things at Once: 10 Easy Steps to Organized Living—it was a work of genius! Hilary had been reading it for two days now, and had gotten through enough of it to know that life didn't have to be as messy and chaotic as it always was around their house.

Hilary brushed her curly red hair out of her face, and glanced across the room at her father, who was busily putting the dinner dishes into the dishwasher.

Her dad was so hopeless, Hilary thought, shaking her head sympathetically. So totally inefficient. Look at him, taking a year with each dish, rinsing it carefully before placing it in precise position in the dishwasher.

As soon as she finished the book, Hilary told herself, she would show her dad how to live his life better, more effectively, less wastefully. He would be so grateful. . . .

Mom, too. Here she came now, clearing some more dishes off the table, and giving Hilary a look. It was a familiar look, the

"Why don't you stop what you're doing and help out a little" look.

Mrs. Lighter went over to the dishwasher and put the dishes down on the counter. "Larry, honey," she said, "do you think you could hurry it up a little with those dishes?" She started putting bowls into the dishwasher any old way, helping her husband get the job done quickly.

He gently put a hand on her arm to stop her. Then he took out the dishes she'd just put in, and placed them back on the counter. "Kate, *honey*," he said with a tight little smile, "there is a right way and a wrong way to put dishes in the dishwasher—and the right way takes a little more time."

He gestured toward the perfectly arranged rack. "You see these slots?" he asked. "They're different sizes for a reason: to optimize the use of space."

Hilary's mom took a cup and deliberately placed it in the wrong spot. "*Honey*, they're *dishes*," she said, putting her hands on her hips, and sounding annoyed now. "You don't have to put them in perfectly. As long as they get clean, who cares?"

What a joke! thought Hilary, looking up at the two of them over the top of her book. She had kept her mouth shut as long as she could, but she couldn't take another second of this nonsense.

"Hel-lo?" she interrupted. "Here's an idea. Mom, *you* rinse and stack. Dad, *you* load 'em in the dishwasher. Nobody gets in anybody's way! Teamwork, y'know?"

Ta-da! Surely now, they'd both fall to their knees in gratitude.

But her dad just gave her a tolerant smile. "That's great, sweetheart," he said, going back to stacking dishes, "but we've got it under control."

Hilary looked to her mom. Surely *she* would be a little more receptive to her advice?

"Yeah, don't worry," her mom said. "We've been doing this a long time."

Like they'd learned one single thing about efficiency in all those years, Hilary thought disgustedly. She heaved a long sigh.

If only they would read this book, she thought. But of course she knew they wouldn't. Not if she suggested it. Because as far as they were concerned, what did she know? When were they going to get it? Hilary was the brains of this family!

She decided to show them a thing or two. "Well," she said, "maybe there's a better way to do it? Look, washing the dishes is a simple matter of organization. No different than running a home." Hilary sat back and folded her arms in front of her.

"Oh-ho!" Her parents raised their eyebrows in unison. "And, uh, *you* know something about running a home?" her mom asked dubiously. She gave her husband a wink and a smile.

"Maybe you'd like to show us how well you could run a home?" he suggested. Her mom cracked up, laughing hysterically at the thought of Hilary trying to run things.

That did it. Hilary was not one to shrink from a challenge. "What?" she said, staring right back at them. "I could manage this place with my eyes closed!"

"Uh-huh . . ." her dad said with a disbelieving smile.

Hilary's eyes narrowed with determination. "You don't think I can do it?" She saw her mom bite down on her lip to keep from laughing out loud again.

"Did I say that?" her dad asked, playing innocent.

"No, you didn't say that," her mom said.

"You *don't* think I can do it!" Hilary said, pointing an accusing finger at them as she rose from her chair. "All right, you're on! I'll handle the whole house. For a week! I'll bet you two tickets to the Ricky Martin concert!"

"Okeydokey," her dad said, putting an arm around his wife.

"This ought to be interesting," her mom said cheerfully.

"It'll be a breeze," Hillary assured them.

A trace of uncertainty shivered through Hilary as her parents left the kitchen. For a moment, she regretted her offer, but she shook the feeling off. Hey, she could do this. Everything would be fine, and they'd *have* to respect her, once she'd showed them how it was done.

Taking a deep breath, she walked over to the dishwasher and started stacking. Those two tickets to the Ricky Martin concert were as good as hers.

Morgan sure was glad to have Hilary around. At least there was one other girl she knew in this town. Not that there was anything wrong with Elliott or Coleman. And she got along with Nick most of the time. But when she and Nick had a fight, like now, or when Nick and the other boys were acting immature in the way only boys can, it was great to have another girl as a friend.

Of course, Morgan and Hilary weren't anything alike. Hilary wasn't into sports at all, and while Morgan liked a good movie as much as anybody, reading subtitles at the foreign films Hilary liked just wasn't Morgan's thing. Still, Hilary was really nice, and easy to talk to—*most* of the time.

Today, Hilary seemed kind of distracted. Her mind was obviously on this deal she'd made with her mom and dad. Morgan thought it was kind of a dumb bargain. She knew *she* would never have agreed to it, not even to see Ricky Martin. On the other hand, Morgan wouldn't mind a bit if Hilary won, and then invited her to go to the concert with her.

"Dishes done . . . vacuuming done . . ." Hilary muttered to herself as she and Morgan speed-walked down the driveway.

Hilary's usual walk was more leisurely.

To her, exercise normally meant an hour talking on the phone. But something had obviously changed since yesterday, Morgan decided. Hilary was like a different person, so fast and efficient. Morgan had come over to complain about Nick, but she hadn't gotten a word in edgewise: Hilary chattered away as she did chore after chore.

So when Hilary asked Morgan to come speed-walking with her, Morgan was more than happy to agree. There were some things she wanted to get off her chest. And if anybody knew how stupid Nick could be, it had to be his sister, Hilary.

"Nick is being such a jerk," Morgan complained. "He is impossible to work with!"

"Bathroom tomorrow . . ." Hilary mumbled, swinging her arms as they turned the corner at the end of the block.

"Hilary!" Morgan said.

"Oh, sorry." Hilary checked her watch. "Talk faster, Morgan," she said. "I have exactly eleven minutes left before I have to start doing laundry."

Morgan sighed in exasperation.

"Sorry, sorry," Hilary said, breathing harder now as their pace got faster. "You were saying?"

"If it's not his idea, then it's no good," Morgan told her. "Well, you know, that's just fine with me. Let him do all the work, if he's so smart."

"Someone has to take charge," Hilary pointed out with a self-satisfied smile and a shrug.

What? Was she siding with Nick? "I have no problem with somebody taking charge," Morgan explained. "It's when they take *over* that it bugs me."

"My mom and dad couldn't even load the dishwasher without making a huge deal out of it," Hilary said. "They needed *me* to step in. Help organize."

Morgan looked at Hilary in disbelief. How could she be so oblivious to what Morgan was saying?

"I guess 'stepping in' runs in the family," Morgan commented. She was sure her little dig would go right over Hilary's head, and she was right.

"I guess so," Hilary said cheerfully.

Like brother, like sister, Morgan thought sadly. Nick and Hilary were definitely not team players!

CHAPTER FOUR

FLYING SOLO

The more he thought about it, the happier Nick felt. It was all for the best that the others had opted out of their group project. This way, he wouldn't have to put up with all their interruptions. Honestly, how many dumb ideas was he supposed to listen to, when in two seconds, he could come up with the perfect solution himself?

He began on Sunday, the morning after the big blowup. Since it was such a nice day, Nick decided that he'd work on the patio table. He grabbed some poster board from the den and tucked it under his arm to take it outside. "Stencils: check. Scissors . . . where are the scissors? They were here yesterday. . . ."

Nick ran into the kitchen, where his mom was preparing a light snack of raw veggies and dip. She looked more relaxed than Nick had seen her in months, humming softly as she cut the cucumbers.

"Mom, Scissors?" he asked, already pulling drawers open and scattering stuff around as he looked for them.

His mom reached over with her right hand, opened a drawer, grabbed a pair of scissors, and held them up for Nick without missing a beat.

"Mom, this project's going to be great!" Nick said excitedly as he took the scissors from her. "A guaranteed A!"

His mom made a face. "I thought this was supposed to be a 'group' project," she said sarcastically.

"Well, the 'group' can't keep up." Nick ran out of the room, then realized he didn't have everything he needed, and ran back in. "Magazines!" he said breathlessly. "I need magazines!" On the table, he spotted one. "Hey, Mom, can I cut this one up?"

"Not that one!" his mom said, shaking her head. "I've been saving it for an article. How about that one over there? And please make sure you put the scissors back when you're done."

"Let the brilliance begin!" Nick cried happily, grabbing his dad's *Sports Weekly* and heading into the living room.

His dad was sitting there on the sofa,

watching a comedy on TV. He was laughing softly to himself, with his feet up on the coffee table and a bag of popcorn in his hand.

"Ah, relaxation," he said as Nick barreled across the room behind him.

"Hey, Dad," Nick said, thinking of something else he was missing. "Have you seen the glue around here?"

His dad's face took on a thoughtful expression, but he didn't take his gaze off the TV screen. "What kind of glue?" he asked. "Wood glue? Epoxy? Rubber cement? What?"

Nick rolled his eyes. "Glue glue, Dad," he said, spelling it out for him. "You know, the white stuff?"

His dad nodded. "Top drawer, left of the sink," he said, still glued to the tube.

Nick's mom came into the room with her

snack and plopped down next to her husband on the couch. They gave each other affectionate smiles and munched away.

Nick crossed in front of the sofa on the way to the stairs, and noticed that there were some markers on the coffee table. He stopped to grab them.

"This for your project?" his dad asked, craning his neck to see around Nick.

"Yeah," Nick replied, struggling to hold on to his entire load of stuff.

Nick's dad shook his head. "I can't believe that your buddies bailed on you, and left you on your own."

Nick shrugged, as if to say, "Who cares?"

"Not even Morgan wanted to help?" his mom asked, puzzled.

"Oh . . ." Nick said, taken aback. Ever since she'd moved here, Morgan had always been eager to help with *everything*. How could Nick explain to his mom that Morgan's helpful side was sometimes a real pain?

"Yeah," he said. "What are you going to do? But it's cool," he assured both of them, backing toward the hall. "I work much better alone anyway."

Nick bounded out of the den, through the kitchen, and onto the patio, leaving his parents to enjoy their "time off." He had some serious work to do. . . .

Hilary danced around the floor of the laundry room and into the kitchen to the beat of a Ricky Martin song blaring from the stereo. She glided across the room with two thick wet towels wrapped around her feet and secured with big rubber bands.

While she danced, her toweled feet cleaned and polished the floor. Meanwhile, with her free hands, she took the dirty dishes from the sink and arranged them in the dishwasher.

"Ricky Martin, here I come!" She grabbed Leonardo, the family beagle, and lifted him into the now empty sink for a much-needed bath.

"Multitasking!" she cooed. Hilary was so pleased with herself that she could have burst right there on the spot. She was *so* much more efficient than either of her parents already!

"I'm a lean, mean, cleaning machine!" she cried happily. "And this is only my first day. Just think how much more on top of things I'll be by the end of the week!"

She wiped the countertop, still dancing to the music, then grabbed a basketful of laundry and headed to the laundry room. She threw the clothes hurriedly into the washing machine and turned it on, dancing back into the kitchen in case Leo decided to jump out of the sink to avoid his bath.

She started the dishwasher, then went to the sink and doused Leonardo with warm water. She squirted some shampoo on him, and began scrubbing. She had lathered and rinsed the dog once, and gotten a good second lather going, when the buzzer sounded, telling her the wash was done and ready to be put into the dryer.

Hilary danced across the gleaming, shiny floor, back into the laundry room. She opened the cover of the washing machine—and screamed.

The clothes in the washer had all turned pink!

She fished around for the culprit, and pulled out a red wool sweater. Now, how had *that* gotten in there? Hilary heaved an exasperated sigh. "Oh well . . . I guess I'll have to redo this load . . . with bleach."

She grabbed for a bottle of bleach, and poured some in. She started the washer going again, then turned to head back to the kitchen—and there was Leonardo, covered with suds, staring up at her with his big, eager, puppy-dog eyes. Then he shook himself off—all over her nice, gleaming, polished floor!

"Aaaahhh! Leo! My floor!" She dove for the dog, but missed. Leo shook himself again, and this time, the suds and dirty water went all over Hilary!

"Leo! Look what you did! Eww!" She grabbed him, but Leo slipped through her fingers, sending more suds flying at her.

Then she dove one last time, caught hold of him with both arms, and made sure to hold on. Splayed out on the once shiny floor, Hilary wrinkled up her nose in disgust as Leo's stinky dog-water began to soak through her clothes.

She was about to burst into tears of frustration, but looking up, she saw that her mother had come in, and was staring at her with a look of amusement on her face. "How's it going?" she asked.

"Great!" Hilary said, trying to sound carefree. "Just perfect!" Well, if she'd come in two minutes earlier, it *would* have been! "In fact, Mom, you just relax until dinner," Hilary said, getting in deeper and deeper as she tried to cover for herself. "I'm planning a five-course meal."

"Five courses?" her mom repeated, with her eyes wide. She looked around at the suds-filled room. *"Tonight?"*

Hilary seized the opening. "Uh, no!" she said. *"Tomorrow* night." Oh, well, at least it bought her twenty-four hours to get a feast together. "Tonight, I thought we'd have . . ." Hilary fell silent, drawing a complete blank.

"Leftovers?" her mother suggested helpfully.

"Great!" Hilary cried, feeling relieved.

Her mom smiled, gave Hilary a little pat on the shoulder for encouragement, and walked out of the room.

Hilary sank back down onto the floor in exhaustion. Why had she gone and offered to make a five-course meal? "Stupid!" she told herself.

At least she still had the book. Sure—the book! What was I worried about? thought Hilary, laughing at how panicked she'd been just a moment before.

So what if she'd had a little setback? She could get back in control of things. After all, how hard could it really be to throw together a nice dinner? If Mom and Dad could do it, so could she—and better!

CHAPTER FIVE

PROJECT IMPOSSIBLE

"This isn't working."

Nick sat on the floor in the middle of his bedroom, surrounded by the torn-up remains of posters he'd started, then given up on. He'd had five false starts already—ideas that seemed great in his head, but looked totally lame on poster board.

For each try, he'd gone through piles of magazines, cutting out pictures for collages. He'd used up most of his markers, glue, and glitter, not to mention the fact that he had only one piece of poster board left, and it was bright yellow.

He was sunk. Finito. Kaput. History. He was going to get them all an F—and all because his friends had abandoned him!

There was a soft knock on the door. "Who's there?" Nick called weakly, still staring numbly at the wreckage of his project.

The door opened, and Coleman came in. "'Sup, man? How's it going?" he asked.

"Great!" Nick chirped, trying to sound cheerful. "Couldn't be better!"

'Slaw took a slow look around the room, then back at Nick. He raised one eyebrow doubtfully at the sorry-looking piece of yellow poster board Nick was holding. "Yeah. Couldn't be worse, you mean," he said, laughing.

Nick was about to ask Coleman what was so funny, when his mom came in through the open door. "Nick, phone," she said, holding out the cordless. "It's Morgan."

Nick made a disgusted face. *Now* she was calling him? *Now?* After putting him through a whole day of torture?

She was probably calling just to torment him. Well, no way was he going to give her the satisfaction of seeing him beaten—no matter how much he needed her help!

"Mom, I'm busy," he explained coolly, indicating 'Slaw. "Could you take a message?"

"Yeah, Mrs. Lighter," Coleman said, "Look how busy he's been. Look at his progress!" Laughing some more, he held up the blank yellow piece of poster board.

"Please, Mom?" Nick begged.

His mom gave him a long, disapproving look, then handed him the phone and walked out of the room without saying a word.

Nick took a deep breath, composing himself, then shot a brief glance at Coleman before putting the phone to his ear. "Hello?" he said, doing his best imitation of a happy camper.

He was sure she was about to ask him how it was going, whether he was finished yet, and what he had come up with. Nick could feel the cold sweat breaking out all over him as he wracked his brain for a convincing response.

But he needn't have bothered. Morgan wasn't interested in what he was doing. As usual, thought Nick, she was all wrapped up in herself. "Hey," she said. "I've got a great idea. We do a chess game—Thomas Jefferson on one side, and King George on the other. . . ."

Nick cut her off. "Yeah, I thought of that, too. Just doesn't feel right." It was true. Nick *had* thought of a chess game, but had rejected it before even trying it out on poster board. A chess game wasn't that original, he had felt. It was a safe B, but had no chance of getting them an A for originality.

"Anyway," he lied, "I'm almost finished."

He shot a glance at Coleman, who was looking from Nick to the empty poster board and back again. "Nick, what are you talking about?" he said.

"Shhh!" Nick commanded, putting a finger to his lips and indicating the phone.

"Whatever," Coleman told Nick, shaking his head in amusement. "I'm outta here. Good luck tomorrow." He stopped at the door, and shook his head one more time as a grin spread over his face. "And I do mean luck!" he added in a whisper, and left.

"See you later, 'Slaw!" Nick called after him, loud enough for Morgan to hear. "Glad you liked it!" Then he put the phone back to his ear. "Yeah, Morgan?" he said, with as much false confidence as he could muster. "Just be ready to thank me tomorrow when Mr. Chambers gives us an A."

He hung up, then swallowed hard. It was already 8:30. He had to come up with something, and fast!

"Great job, Nick. It's everything you said, and less." Morgan shook her head in sad disbelief as she stared at the sorry excuse for a poster Nick had created in all their names.

"A C-minus?" Elliott moaned, staring at the big red mark Mr. Chambers had drawn at the top of the poster.

"Your teacher must have been feeling generous," Coleman said, holding up the poster and laughing.

Other kids were coming out of school, passing them, and giggling as they looked at Nick's pathetic "masterpiece." It showed George Washington crossing the Delaware, standing up in the boat and throwing a football toward a goalpost. In plain black stenciled letters—no glitter, no colored markers—it read, GOOD-BYE, OLD ENGLAND! HELLO, NEW ENGLAND—JOIN THE PATRIOTS!

Morgan pointed at the poster. "One

minor historical fact you seemed to over-look: football wouldn't be invented for an-other hundred years!"

"It's not about football!" Nick protested weakly.

"Then why is George Washington throwing a Hail Mary pass?" Morgan wanted to know.

Nick gave them all an angry look. "I didn't hear any better ideas from any of you," he complained.

Now it was Elliott's turn to get angry. "How could you hear us?" he asked. "You weren't listening!"

Amen to that! thought Morgan. She was so furious she could have exploded.

"And like my dad's always saying," Elliott went on, "there's no I in 'team.'"

"Yeah," Morgan agreed. "And there's no C in 'history.'"

That set Coleman off, laughing hysterically. "There is now!" he managed to say between spasms of hilarity.

"You wouldn't be laughing if it was your C," Elliott said, giving him an annoyed look.

"Yeah," 'Slaw said, still laughing. "Like that could ever happen!"

The argument continued as the MNFC walked down the street together. Elliott and Coleman veered right at the corner of Tremont, but Morgan and Nick were still yelling at each other as they turned in at the Lighters' driveway, where Nick's dad was unloading shopping bags from the trunk of the car.

Nick was still going on and on about how they'd all let him down. Morgan shook her head in frustration. Can't Nick see what a jerk he's being? she thought.

"I take on all the responsibility," Nick was saying, "and now everybody's freaked when we don't get an A-plus-plus."

"No," she corrected him, "we're mad because you totally took over and got us a C-minus-minus!"

Mr. Lighter cleared his throat. "Maybe your teacher wanted you to find a way to work *with* each other," he said, giving each of them one handle of a heavy grocery bag to carry inside. "Like a team? Hmmm?"

Morgan gave Nick a bitter look, and he shot it right back at her. She and Nick on the same team? Yeah, right! After this disaster, it didn't seem likely to happen again.

CHAPTER SIX

THE MAGIC JERSEY STRIKES

The moment Hilary had gotten home from school, she'd started making preparations for her big five-course dinner. She knew now that she'd been a fool to think she could handle the whole household by herself for a week, without even finishing the book first. She'd barely made it through yesterday at all. Today, though, she wanted to make up for everything. She had stayed up till two in the morning reading in bed until she'd finished the book. And now she was ready. This meal was going to be perfect—a thing of beauty, a joy to behold.

She sat at the head of the table, trying to figure out how to knot the linen napkins so they would look pretty. The diagram in the book hadn't been very helpful at all.

She looked up at her handiwork, and she had to give herself an A for table-setting. The plates, glasses, candlesticks, and silverware were all laid out beautifully on the family's best tablecloth. Even so, she knew she couldn't waste much time on napkins—not with a five-course dinner to prepare by six o'clock!

She heard her dad's car pulling into the driveway with the groceries she'd sent him for, and then Morgan's and Nick's voices as they came inside. Good! Hilary was going to need some help from her brother and cousin if she was going to impress Mom and Dad with this fancy dinner.

Her dad came in, and stopped dead at the doorway. "Wow!" he exclaimed. "Hilary, look at this table! How did you do it?"

Hilary could feel herself blushing with pride. "Simple," she said, flashing him a calm smile. "Time management."

He studied the settings, and a puzzled expression came over his face. "Er, why is the table set for eight?" he asked.

Hilary blushed again, this time from embarrassment. She hadn't been thinking when she'd done the place settings. The picture in the book showed a table set for eight, and she'd just copied it exactly!

"Um . . . it looks prettier that way," she fudged.

Her dad shrugged, and smiled, and Hilary smiled back, glad to see that he'd bought her lame explanation.

Just then her mom came in from the den. "It's beautiful," she complimented Hilary, admiring the table.

Hilary blushed all over again, thrilled that she'd made such a good impression. All her failures of the day before had been forgotten. A great dinner tonight, and the rest of the week's meals would be smooth sailing. She could probably get by on burgers and frozen vegetables.

"Ready, honey?" her dad asked her mom.

"Let's go," her mom said.

"Wait a second!" Hilary said. "Where are you going?"

"Just out," her mom explained.

Suddenly, panic welled up inside Hilary. What did she mean, they were "just going out"? Her mom and dad never did that!

Hilary swallowed hard. "What about dinner?"

"Don't worry," her dad assured her. "We'll be back. Just have to run a few errands."

"Oh," Hilary said, calming down a little. "All right—but dinner starts at six P.M. sharp!"

"We'll be here," her dad said with a smile.

"Wouldn't miss it," her mom added. Locking their arms, they sauntered out of the room. As they went, Hilary overheard her mom saying, "Maybe we can get her to do this every night!"

The sound of her parents' carefree

laughter echoed in Hilary's ears after they'd gone. Now, she had to deliver, or they'd never let her live it down!

Nick was still upset by all the things his friends had said to him. Wasn't it bad enough they'd gotten a C- on their big project? Did they have to make him feel worse on top of it?

It was all Morgan's fault, he told himself as he put away the groceries, careful to avoid talking to her. If she hadn't turned Elliott and Coleman against him, everything would have been okay.

He was glad when Morgan finished up and went into the dining room to say hello to Hilary. Nick headed upstairs to his room. He felt like burying his head in his pillow, and not coming down again till dinner.

THE JERSEY

Walking through the den on his way to the stairs, his attention was caught by the baseball announcer's voice on the TV. Someone must have left the television on, although Nick couldn't imagine who. His dad had been out at the supermarket, and his mom never watched ESPN.

"It's a rare Monday afternoon game between the Braves and the Dodgers today," the announcer was saying, "and we've got quite a pitching matchup. Kevin Brown of the Dodgers will be up against Braves ace Kevin Millwood. . . ."

Suddenly, Nick froze in his tracks. There, draped over the back of the sofa, as if it were watching the game, was the magic jersey his grandfather had left him.

It was made out of heavy, scratchy wool, yellow with blue stripes on the cuffs and arms, and a big blue letter *H* on the front. It was old, and tattered, and *ugly*.

Nick hadn't even wanted the jersey at first. He'd had his eye on his grandpa's old football instead, the one autographed by the 1967 Green Bay Packers, winners of the very first Super Bowl. But unbelievably, Grandpa had chosen to leave the precious football to Morgan—after all those times he and Nick had tossed it around together! It had made Nick angry and jealous just thinking about it. How could Grandpa have given her the football, and him the crummy old jersey?

But after Nick put on the jersey for the first time, he changed his mind entirely. All of a sudden, magical things started to happen. Nick was instantly transformed into Steve Young of the San Francisco 49ers! There he was in the middle of a real

NFL game, and to all the other players, he *was* Young! The magical transformation only lasted a few minutes, but boy, was it spectacular! Nick won that game for his team, using an old, forgotten play of Grandpa's that Morgan had told him about. After that, Nick didn't mind having Morgan in the MNFC.

He'd even told Morgan about the jersey. He'd told *all* his pals, but they didn't believe him—not until they tried it on for themselves! Now, they were all in on the big secret. And it *was* a secret. None of them had told anyone outside of their club. Nick knew that his parents and Hilary wouldn't understand.

But how had the jersey ended up on the sofa? Nick wondered. He kept it on a shelf in the den, along with some other sports memorabilia. Surely it hadn't climbed down off the shelf and walked over to the sofa on its own! No, he thought, growing angrier by the minute. It might be a magic jersey, but as far as Nick knew, it wasn't able to get up and walk on its own.

No . . . Someone had touched it. In spite of the fact that he'd warned everyone in the family never to touch it without his permission, someone had gone and thrown it over the back of the couch.

Well, someone was going to pay! Pushing up his sleeves, Nick grabbed the jersey and marched toward the dining room.

"Wow, Hil," Morgan was saying as the two girls stood together in the dining room. "This looks great. You even hauled out the teeny-tiny forks!"

Hilary gave her an embarrassed smile. She'd set the table in such a hurry, she hadn't even noticed the size of the forks.

"What are they for, anyway?" Morgan asked.

"They're for . . . teeny-tiny bites!" Hilary fudged, with a giggle and a shrug. Then she took the fork from Morgan and put it back where it belonged. "Now, I could use a little help—"

At that very moment, however, Nick burst into the room. "Who's been messing with my jersey?" he demanded. Coming over to Hilary, he looked her right in the eye.

Hilary made a face. "Get real," she said. "I wouldn't touch that ratty old thing with *your* hands!"

Apparently, Nick believed her, because he turned away and marched up to Morgan.

"It wasn't me!" Morgan exclaimed, backing away.

Nick turned away from her, deep in thought. Then he caught sight of the crackers and dip Hilary had already placed on the table. Tucking the jersey under one arm, he reached out for the food with his free hand.

Hilary grabbed Nick's hand by the wrist. "Don't even think about it," she ordered.

"You should let *Nick* help you," Morgan said to Hilary. "I'm sure Uncle Larry and Aunt Kate would appreciate a C-minus dinner!"

Nick wheeled around to face Morgan. "See if I ever help you again, Morgan!" he shouted.

"What a threat!" Morgan shot back sarcastically. "If you hadn't helped out, we might have gotten an A!"

THE JERSEY

Hilary shook her head and sighed, turning away from their childish argument. She had real work to do. Hmmm . . . she thought, looking over the table once more, I think the crystal water pitcher would look better.

She went into the kitchen to get it, and filled it with water and ice. When she came back into the dining room, Morgan and Nick each had a hold of one sleeve of the old jersey and were trying to tug it away from the other.

"Morgan, let go!" Nick was yelling. "I'm going to put it away."

"I'm just looking at it!" Morgan shouted back, giving the jersey another tug. As she did, she rammed right into Hilary's elbow. The blow sent the full pitcher of water flying through the air!

With a scream, Hilary leaped across the

table and grabbed the crystal pitcher before it hit the floor. As she landed, she sensed a flash of blue light, and heard a strange whooshing sound. Wow, thought Hilary. She had come down so hard she was seeing stars!

And look at this mess! Hilary gasped in dismay. Water and ice cubes were everywhere. The beautiful tablecloth was soaked. And all the linen napkins she'd knotted up so carefully—she was going to have to throw everything in the dryer and start all over again!

Thank goodness none of the plates or glasses had been broken, and she'd saved the pitcher with her desperate leap and grab. But Hilary knew she was going to need Morgan and Nick's help to recover from this horrible setback they'd caused her.

"A little help, please!" Hilary called out, reaching out so they could grab her arm and help her off the table.

Nobody took her hand. Hilary looked around. Nick and Morgan were gone!

"This is going to put me way behind schedule!" Hilary moaned, lifting herself off the table. And where had Nick and Morgan gone, anyway? thought Hilary. It was like they'd disappeared into thin air!

CHAPTER SEVEN

A MAJOR-LEAGUE HEADACHE

Nick felt that familiar tingle, and knew at once that he was being transported by the jersey. His arm went transparent, glowing with blue light; then the glow spread to the rest of his body. In a blinding flash, he felt himself whirling through space on waves of brilliant energy, until . . .

Wham! Nick shuddered with the force of re-entry. He blinked, looked around, and saw that he was standing on a pitcher's mound, in a baseball stadium filled with tens of thousands of screaming fans.

They were screaming at *him*, he realized. But who in the world *was* he?

Nick looked back at the fielders behind him. They were dressed in the uniforms of the Atlanta Braves. No, wait a minute— they *were* the Atlanta Braves! The actual team—and he had to be their pitcher. . . .

Nick thought back to what the TV announcer had been saying at the moment he'd found the jersey . . . Holy Mackerel: he was Kevin Millwood!

But wait a minute—where was Morgan? Nick distinctly remembered that she'd been holding the jersey, too. Had she been left behind? Or had she been transported along with him?

The crowd began to boo, and Nick suddenly realized that he was supposed to throw a pitch. He didn't have the faintest idea what to throw.

The catcher called a time-out, got up, and jogged to the mound. There he was, two feet away, looking right at Nick!

"Wow! I can't believe it! Eddie Perez!" Nick gasped.

The catcher took off his mask and looked Nick over. "Nick? Is that you?"

One second, Morgan had been tugging at the jersey in the Lighters' dining room. Then, she too had seen the flash of light, and the next thing she knew, she was crouched behind the plate in full catcher's gear, with a speeding baseball coming straight for her head.

Instinctively, she threw the glove up to protect herself. The ball exploded into the mitt with savage force.

"Ow!" Morgan cried out. Only then did she have time to look up. Suddenly, she realized where she was—and fell right back onto her backside in surprise. The batter, Gary Sheffield, was staring down at her! Gary Sheffield, star home-run hitter of the Los Angeles Dodgers!

"You okay?" he asked, leaning on his bat.

"Uh . . ." Morgan stared back at him, speechless. "I'll . . . I'll be right back." She got up, signaled to the ump for time, and ran out to the mound. Kevin Millwood was waiting there for her—but his facial expression and his stance looked strangely familiar to Morgan.

"Wow! I can't believe it! Eddie Perez!" the pitcher said, gawking at Morgan.

"Nick? Is that you?" she tried.

"M-Morgan? Y-you're Eddie Perez?"

It *was* him! Morgan gave him a cold stare. "Nice going, genius. Now see what you've done?"

"Me?" Nick shouted. "Morgan, this is all your fault!"

"You jumped us both here!" Morgan hissed furiously, pointing an accusing finger at him. "What're we supposed to do now?"

She could hear the fans screaming at them. Above the Braves dugout, she spotted one fan with his face painted in Braves colors. The guy was waving a rubber hatchet. "Come on! Strike him out! Let's go!" he yelled.

Next to him stood a guy with a Dodger hat on. "Whatsamatter, Millwood? Y'afraid to pitch it?" he bellowed.

"We'll be right there!" Nick hollered back at the fans.

Now the umpire was running toward them. "You guys think you might wanna play baseball sometime today?" he shouted. "Come on! Play ball!"

Morgan turned to Nick, furious. "Hilary is expecting us for dinner, and your parents are coming home at six!" she reminded him.

"My wife's expecting me at five-thirty!" the umpire called sarcastically. "Let's go!"

"Yeah . . . we're on it," Nick assured the umpire, waving him back to the plate with his mitt.

It was all too much. Morgan felt the angry tears coming, the tightening feeling in her throat. "I cannot be on a team with you!" she shouted. "I wanna go home!"

"Looks like you don't have much

choice," Nick answered, looking directly at her.

Morgan returned his gaze. She knew it was true. For the moment, at least, they were going to have to act like teammates.

Hilary knew she had no time to waste, especially since Morgan and Nick had left her there to get everything done by herself. She gathered up the wet tablecloth and napkins, and ran through the kitchen to the laundry area. But as she was putting the wet things into the dryer, she saw that her own dirty footprints had somehow gotten all over the tablecloth!

"What did I do?" she gasped. "I must have been in such a hurry that—" Now she'd have to wash everything again first, and then dry it. Since the tablecloth and napkins didn't make a full load, Hilary stuffed a few bath towels in, along with her terrycloth bathrobe. "As long as there's nothing red in there," she muttered.

She poured in the soap—extra soap to get rid of the grimy footprints—and set the washer going. Hilary checked her watch. A quarter to five. She could still have everything ready by six—*barely*.

She finished preparing the main dish— Chicken Francese—and went to work on her sauces, which needed time to simmer. Soon she had things cooking on two burners and in the oven. She popped some slices of garlic bread into the toaster oven and turned it on. She cleaned up the countertops and opened the dishwasher to put the utensils in. "Hmmm," she said, noticing how full it was. "I'd better do a load now. Then I can empty it before we eat, and have it ready for the dinner dishes."

So she put in some dishwashing liquid and turned it on, too.

"There!" she said. "See? I didn't need any help after all. I'm doing fine all by myself!"

A faint, nagging feeling was making her uneasy. What had she forgotten?

"The dog! Walk the dog!" Hilary slapped her hands together, pleased with herself for remembering. "Leo! Where are you? Leo?"

Funny. He usually came right away whenever anyone called him. Then Hilary noticed that the door to the driveway had been left open. "Oh, no!" she cried. "He must have gotten out!" She ran outside, calling, "Leo! Leo? Here, boy!"

"Play ball!" the umpire called. Morgan trotted back to the plate, her heart pounding a mile a minute.

THE JERSEY

She crouched down, glanced up at Gary Sheffield, and thought, You don't give Gary Sheffield a pitch to hit. She signaled Nick for a curveball outside.

Nick shook her off. What was wrong with him? Morgan wondered, frustrated beyond belief. It was just like the history project. Nick never listened to Morgan's opinion.

Okay, then—she flashed him the sign for a change-up. Again, he shook her off. Steaming, Morgan called time, pulled off her catcher's mask, and trotted out to the mound again.

The crowd was booing even louder now. "Hey, we didn't pay to watch you guys talk all day!" the body-painted fan was yelling. "Millwood throws the fastball. Blow it by him, baby!"

It was so loud in the stadium that

Morgan could barely hear herself yelling at Nick. "Why did you bring me here if you're not gonna throw what I call?"

Nick held his arms out in protest. "I didn't bring you anywhere!" he insisted. "And right now, I'm trying to figure out how to strike out Gary Sheffield."

Morgan screwed up her face in disbelief. "You can't strike out Gary Sheffield," she said, stating the obvious. "*Nobody* can strike out Gary Sheffield!"

"*I* can," Nick said, calmly staring back at her.

"Errrgh! You are such an egomaniac!" Morgan exploded. "Walk him, like everybody else does!"

"I can't, 'Eddie,'" Nick said, giving her a meaningful glance. "Because *I'm Kevin Millwood*."

"Which, by the way, is no fair," Morgan

said, "because I *love* Kevin Millwood. At least I used to, before he came down with 'Nick-itis.'" She shook her head in disgust. "Amazing. You drive me nuts, no matter who you are!"

Morgan walked back to the plate, still shaking her head. Nick's stubbornness never ceased to amaze her.

She looked up at Gary Sheffield, who was giving her a suspicious glance. "Hey, Gary," she told him, "see that pitcher out there? Get ready, buddy, because he's planning on striking you out."

Sheffield cocked his head to one side in surprise. Then, a slow grin came over his face, and he set himself in the batter's box, just waiting for that big, fat fastball. . . .

CHAPTER EIGHT

PANIC TIME!

Elliott and Coleman knocked and knocked, but nobody answered the door at the Lighters' house. "That's weird," Elliott said. "It's five-thirty in the afternoon. Somebody should be home."

Coleman tried the door, and it opened. "Hellooo?" he called. "Anybody home?"

"Nick? Morgan?" Elliott shouted. There was no answer. Turning to Coleman, he said, "'Slaw, check the den."

THE JERSEY

Coleman peeked into the room. The TV was on: the Braves were playing the Dodgers, and Gary Sheffield was at the plate. Coleman loved Gary Sheffield, and he was tempted to sit down and watch the at-bat. But he kept his attention on the task at hand.

Where could everybody have gone? Coleman looked around, and there, on the trophy shelf, he found his answer. Missing from its usual place was Nick's magic jersey.

'Slaw rushed back out into the hallway. "They're gone," he said to Elliott. "And so is the jersey."

Elliott raised his eyebrows. "Hmm," he said. "I guess they made up." Then he wrinkled up his nose, sniffing a new smell in the air.

'Slaw sniffed, too. Yup, there was no doubt about it. . . .

PANIC TIME!

"Food!" they yelled at once. High-fiving each other, they marched toward the kitchen, with big smiles of anticipation on their faces.

"Bad doggie!" Hilary scolded Leo as she carried him home in her arms. "Mr. Scopes is not going to like it when he sees you dug up all his flowers!"

As she came back into the kitchen, Leo squirmed out of her arms and went running off. She turned to check her simmering sauces, and screamed when she saw Nick's friends, Elliott and Coleman, dipping pieces of sliced garlic bread into her beautiful Francese sauce!

"Aaahhh! Hel-lo," she said. "The only thing worse than having you around is having you eat my food! Good-bye!"

She was about to shoo them out the

kitchen door, when she heard a rumbling sound coming from the direction of the laundry room. Hilary ran over to find the washer rocking violently, objecting to its huge, unbalanced load. Worse, she'd put too much soap in, and there were suds everywhere.

Hilary was knee-deep in them. She reached to shut off the machine, and just then, the hose popped loose from the back of the washer, spraying her with a jet of cold water.

"Ugh!" Hilary screamed. She managed to pull the plug before the room flooded entirely. Then, drenched and shaking the suds off herself, she made her way back into the kitchen to make sure Nick's friends hadn't ransacked the food while she was gone.

Smoke! There was smoke pouring from

the toaster oven! Hilary screamed again and turned it off. As Elliott and Coleman looked on, she popped out the blackened pieces of garlic bread, and juggled them like hotcakes all the way to the garbage can. Just then, the blender top popped off, and her homemade strawberry smoothie went spraying all over the kitchen!

The pots were boiling over. The dishwasher was making strange noises. And the blender was shooting sparks.

In desperation, Hilary reached for the blender plug and pulled—and the whole house went dark.

There was a long silence, and then, one word was spoken in unison by three different voices: "Uh-oh."

From behind the plate, sixty feet, six inches from the mound, Morgan could see the beads of sweat rolling down Nick's face. Well, he was right to be nervous, she thought. It was him the fans were screaming at, urging him on as he threw fastball after fastball to that great fastball hitter, Gary Sheffield, trying—against her advice, as usual—to strike him out.

He wasn't doing too badly, either. He'd actually blown one fastball right by Sheffield. Another fastball had been fouled back, missed by just a fraction of an inch. Nick had been lucky that one hadn't been hit for a home run.

The near miss must have spooked Nick, because he threw the next two fastballs outside and high. Now, the count was two and two.

Morgan knew Gary Sheffield was set up for the breaking ball. He'd seen four fastballs in a row. Even if he was expecting the slider, he wouldn't be able to adjust well enough to make good contact.

Morgan thought about putting down two fingers to signal the slider. But she knew what Nick's reaction would be.

So fine, she thought. She put down one finger, for the fastball. If Gary Sheffield hit it out of the park, Nick would have only himself to blame.

Still, Morgan didn't really want Nick to fail. After all, like it or not, they were teammates now. If he lost the game, she lost too. So, since she knew Nick wouldn't listen to her advice, Morgan decided to help him in another way, by psyching out the batter.

"So—two and two," she said to Sheffield, who was set up at the plate, waiting for the pitch. "It looks like Mr. Super Batter is behind in the count."

Sheffield blinked, confused and distracted. "Two and two means I'm even," he told her, trying to keep his focus on Nick. "*One* and two, I'm behind."

"Are you sure?" Morgan needled him.

"Yeah," Sheffield said, then wavered. "At least, I'm *pretty* sure. . . ."

The pitch left Nick's hand, and Sheffield swung. *Crack!* The ball sailed down the right field line—and foul. Morgan's distraction tactic had worked; it had made Sheffield's swing just a split second late.

"Tough to strike me out, throwing like that," Sheffield told her, shaking his head and smiling.

Morgan smiled right back at him through her catcher's mask. "We're not about to walk you, if that's what you're thinking," she said.

PANIC TIME!

Crouching back down, she signaled Nick for yet another fastball, this time on the inside corner. Nick threw it, right to the mitt. Boy, he sure is good, Morgan thought. She'd caught Nick before, but he was a much better pitcher as Kevin Millwood.

Sheffield swung, and fouled a screaming line drive into the stands along the third baseline. Fans ducked for cover.

Morgan smiled, satisfied with her pitch call. Sheffield had swung early this time, making up for what had happened on the previous pitch. But Morgan had crossed him up by calling for the pitch inside.

Now Morgan and Nick had run out of tricks to disguise the fastball. Sheffield would be sure to cream the next one. It was time for the slider, and Nick had just better realize it.

Morgan called for time, and trotted out

to the mound. She pulled off the mask, and wiped the sweat from her brow. Nick took off his cap and did the same. In the stands, the fans were getting restless again.

"Get me out there! I'll sit him down!" screamed the fan with the painted face and the rubber hatchet.

"Let's get this game going!" shouted the Dodger fan next to him.

Morgan tried to shut out their voices, but it was hard to concentrate. She could only imagine what it must be like for Nick.

"The man's a machine!" Nick complained, frustrated.

"Throw the slider," Morgan told him, smiling confidently.

"No way!" Nick cried. "He crushes those. You don't know what you're talking about."

PANIC TIME!

"A slider is also the pitch he whiffs most often," Morgan pointed out. Nick realized that she knew her sports stats better than he did. But would he listen to her? Or would he let his ego get the best of him again?

"What if he doesn't whiff it?" Nick asked, weakening.

"What if he does?" Morgan's eyes widened with excitement. "Nick, we have to work together here," she pleaded. "I can see how Sheffield is standing, and I know what he's thinking! He's not expecting a slider. Throw it."

Nick looked at her anxiously. She gave him a confident nod to perk up his courage, then turned toward home plate.

CHAPTER NINE

MOMENT OF TRUTH

"Eww! What was that?" Hilary had been feeling around in the darkness of the kitchen, and suddenly drew her hand back in fear and disgust. It was something furry and moving! Was it a rat? A raccoon?

"That was my head, thank you," came Elliott's annoyed voice.

Hilary breathed a huge sigh of relief. But of course, it was only momentary relief. It was only another second before she came back to the horrifying reality: the house was a disaster area. She'd be doomed if her parents got back and saw the kitchen like this. That is, if they could see anything at all!

What had she been thinking, to believe she could handle the house for a week all by herself? Her parents could barely do it between them. Hilary promised herself that if she ever got out of this with her reputation intact, she would rip that stupid book to shreds.

There was total darkness in the house. And when the lights came back on, there was going to be a huge mess to clean up. Then there was dinner to get ready, and the table to reset; there was no possible way she could do it all on her own.

"You guys have to help me," she begged, her voice trembling. "Pleeease?"

Her eyes were adjusting slowly to the darkness. She could make out their shapes now, Coleman's big frame standing next to Elliott's smaller one.

It looked like Elliott had his hands on his hips. "Hmmm, I don't know," she heard him say. "I seem to remember someone telling us to leave."

"Oh, come on!" Hilary moaned in desperation. "I've tolerated you guys for years!"

Coleman had found a flashlight in one of the kitchen drawers. He turned it on and shined it right in Hilary's eyes. "What do we get if we help?" he asked.

"Anything!" Hilary promised, putting a hand up to shield her eyes from the glare. "Anything! Please!"

Coleman moved the flashlight beam to his own face. Lit from below, the dark shadows made his smile seem like something out of a horror movie. "Invite us to dinner," he demanded, and the grin grew more hideous.

"Except that," Hilary backed off. The thought of these two gobbling up half the food she'd slaved over all afternoon was too much to bear.

"Okay, then," Elliott said, rubbing his hands together. "How about a kiss?" He waggled his eyes at Hilary in the ghostly glare of Coleman's flashlight.

Hilary grimaced. "Eww! Leonardo wouldn't kiss you!" she told him. "Forget it!"

"Okay . . ." Coleman said casually, shutting off the flashlight. "Let's go, Elliott. We're not wanted here."

"No! Wait!" Hilary stopped them, frantic now. There was no way around it. She could clean up the mess by herself, she could finish dinner and reset the table.

But she had no idea how to fix the electricity and get the lights back on again. And without the lights, she was totally helpless. "Okay. You can eat dinner! Just help me—*now*!" she begged.

The light flashed back on, illuminating Coleman's face, which was now wearing a huge grin. "All right, all right," he said, moving over to the far wall by the laundry room. "Man, this family is bossy."

He shone the flashlight on the wall, revealing a big gray metal box. Hilary had probably passed it a million times and never noticed it. Coleman opened the box's door and flipped a switch. Instantly, the house was lit again.

Hilary was aghast. "You *knew* that's all it was!" she screamed, pointing an accusing finger at Coleman, who was giggling along with Elliott and giving him a

Monday Night Football Club handshake.

"Can I help it if I'm a genius?" Coleman asked, laughing his head off now.

"Well, genius, a deal's a deal," Hilary cornered him. "You guys still have to help me clean up this mess."

She pointed to the boiled-over pot, the spilled smoothie, the soap suds, then put her hands on her hips. "Well?"

Elliott and Coleman looked at each other, their smiles vanishing as they realized what they'd gotten themselves into.

Coleman looked at Elliott and shook his head in dismay. "We've gotta stop coming over here," he said.

"We still haven't seen any baseball! Come on! Pitch!" It was that fan with the painted face again. Nick wondered what it was about his voice that made it stick out from all the others. Something about it made his hair stand on end, and disturbed his concentration.

Nick realized now how hard it was for professional athletes like Kevin Millwood to concentrate with the fans screaming at them all the time. He'd never understood before just how much focus it takes to succeed when the spotlight's on you, and millions of people are watching. As Steve Young, Nick had been too surprised by the jersey's magic to care about the crowd. But here on the baseball diamond, with the tension rising before every pitch, it was impossible to shut out the noise.

Morgan was calling for the slider, just as she said she would. Nick hesitated. Something inside him didn't want to throw the off-speed pitch. It felt too much like giving in to Gary Sheffield. Worse, it meant he'd be giving in to Morgan. It would be like admitting he should have listened to her about the history project, too. It would mean she'd been right all along.

But, if he threw the slider and Gary Sheffield hit it over the fence, it would be all Morgan's fault, just as the C- in history had been all *his* fault. Then they'd be even.

Besides, he knew logically that the slider was the pitch to throw, even though it went against everything he was feeling.

"You'd better be right, Morgan," he muttered. Adjusting his fingers on the ball to the slider grip, Nick went into his windup. He saw Morgan raise the glove; saw Gary Sheffield coil up to swing. He released the ball with a little extra motion, just to make Sheffield react as if it were a fastball coming.

He saw the ball sailing through the air.

Then suddenly, it was as if it were moving in slow motion. His throwing hand glowed blue, and became transparent.

The last thing he saw before he jumped was the ball whizzing by the bat, and landing safely in the glove of Eddie Perez. He heard the faint echo of the umpire's voice shouting, "Stee-rike three! Yer out!"

They'd done it! Together, working as a team, he and Morgan had struck out Gary Sheffield!

Then Nick felt himself being sucked through time and space, spinning in the vortex of the jersey's magic.

Coleman and Elliott were busy setting the table. Coleman placed a bowl full of dinner rolls at the center, where everybody could reach them. The bowl of raw veggies went next to it.

MOMENT OF TRUTH

Meanwhile, Elliott busied himself trying to tie the napkins in knots. Coleman laughed when he saw the puzzled look on his friend's face. "What's the matter?" he asked. "Can't follow simple directions?"

"I'm doing it, I'm doing it," Elliott assured him. "Actually, we got the easy jobs. Hilary's the one who had to clean up all the goop in the kitchen."

"Yeah," Coleman acknowledged. "Not to mention doing the cooking. Mmmm . . . smell that!"

Elliott's expression grew thoughtful. "'Slaw, are you thinking what I'm thinking?" he asked.

Coleman sighed and nodded his head. "Nick and Morgan have been gone a long time," he said.

"I wonder why they jumped without telling us?" Elliott mused.

From the kitchen came the sound of Hilary's voice, yelling, "Aren't you two done yet?"

"I think the answer's obvious," Coleman said, pointing his thumb in Hilary's direction.

Just then, she came into the room, took a look at the unfinished state of the table, and let out a groan of frustration. "Mom and Dad are pulling up in the driveway, and it's not ready! I told them six o'clock!"

She looked like she was about to burst into tears. Elliott went over to her and put a reassuring hand on her shoulder. "Don't panic, Hil. It's okay. The food smells great, and everything's clean. It's as good as . . . as . . . the school cafeteria!"

Hilary grimaced, looking as if she were about to be sick, then snapped out of it with a shake of her shoulders.

MOMENT OF TRUTH

The sound of the front door opening jerked them all to attention. "Hello-o!" came the sound of Mrs. Lighter's voice. "Are we early?"

"We were told not to be late," Mr. Lighter called from the living room.

Hilary started waving her hands in the air, in a state of total panic. She darted from place to place, grabbing the candelabra and putting it on the table, getting the candles and sticking them in the holes.

Meanwhile, Elliott had finished tying his napkins. Now he tossed them, one to each place setting, landing them almost perfectly with uncanny accuracy.

Coleman poured water in all the glasses, making sure not to spill any. He could hear Mr. and Mrs. Lighter in the living room, laughing at a joke Mr.

Lighter must have told. He could see their shadows cross the floor—they were coming! They'd be in the dining room any second.

Just then, there was a sudden *whoosh*, followed by a flash of blue light, and all of a sudden, Nick and Morgan were standing by the head of the table!

"Whoa!" Elliott said, his eyes as wide as saucers.

"You're back!" Coleman said, breathing a sigh of relief. He looked over at Hilary, who was greeting her parents as they came in. None of them had noticed Nick and Morgan's supernatural arrival.

Then Hilary turned around and saw them. "Where've you two been?" she asked, a note of annoyance creeping into her voice.

Nick and Morgan didn't seem to be

bothered by her tone. They were smiling broadly, their faces flushed with excitement. "Just playing a little baseball with Gary Sheffield," Morgan commented, shooting Nick a wink and giving him an MNFC handshake.

Just then, the oven timer went off— *ding!*

"Dinner's ready!" Elliott said, rubbing his hands together in hungry anticipation.

Coleman looked over at Hilary. She had her eyes up to heaven, and was mouthing the silent words, "Thank you!"

"Honey, isn't this beautiful?" Mr. Lighter asked his wife.

"It looks great!" Mrs. Lighter said.

Hilary gave them a pained little smile, then rushed out into the kitchen to take dinner out of the oven. Mr. and Mrs.

THE JERSEY

Lighter followed her, oooing and aahing over everything their daughter had accomplished.

Coleman and Elliott exchanged knowing looks. If Hilary's parents only knew!

CHAPTER TEN

THE SWEET TASTE OF VICTORY

The rest of the meal came off without a hitch. Hilary beamed as she watched them all, eating her food and loving every bite of it. The candles flickered, the crystal glistened, and everyone was in a great mood. Hilary thought again of those Ricky Martin tickets. It would be a piece of cake to earn them now. All she had to do was get through the rest of the week without a major screw-up.

She got up to start clearing the empty plates. As she went around the table, the others pushed themselves back in their chairs, wiped their mouths with their linen napkins, and sighed in satisfaction.

"Um . . . could I have some more water?" Coleman asked Hilary sweetly. Hilary rolled her eyes. He'd been requesting all kinds of service all through dinner, just to get her up out of her seat to serve him, again and again.

Oh, well, she thought. How mad could she be, after he and Elliott had saved her? She put down the dirty dishes, grabbed the water pitcher, and went over to fill his glass, sticking her tongue out at him as she did.

Coleman just laughed. Hilary was opening her mouth to say something when her mom said, "Hilary, you really did it. The house looks great, and dinner was wonderful!"

"Even the service!" her dad agreed. "Right, Coleman?"

Coleman looked up at Hilary and gave her a great big grin. "Couldn't agree more," he said, and laughed again.

Hilary gritted her teeth. It was all she could do not to pour the whole pitcher of ice water over his head.

"Hilary's awesome . . . really," Elliott volunteered, giving her a sincere smile.

Hilary felt her anger vanishing as everyone agreed, giving her a spontaneous round of applause.

"You did such a great job, dessert's on me!" her dad said, getting up from his chair. "Who wants ice cream?"

Everyone cheered, and before Hilary knew it, the room was nearly empty as everyone headed for the family station wagon for a quick trip to the ice cream store.

Elliott was the last to get up and head for the door. Hilary stopped him, putting an arm on his shoulder. "Elliott," she said, "I owe you something." Leaning down toward him, she gave him a little kiss on the cheek.

But to her utter shock and surprise, Elliott seemed less than happy to be kissed. In fact, his face wrinkled up into an expression of sheer horror!

"Eww!" he shrieked. "Ugh!" He started frantically wiping at his face with his hand, then grabbed a linen napkin, dipped it in water, and ran the napkin all over his cheek.

"What?!" Hilary asked, taken aback. "You asked for a kiss."

"It was a *joke*!" he shouted, his eyes

blazing with anger. "Don't you know a joke when you hear one? Ugh! Ugh! 'Slaw!" And with that, he ran out the door, leaving Hilary shaking her head in amazement.

"Boys," she said, sighing and shaking her head. "I'll never understand them as long as I live!"

"Hey, Morgan . . ."

Nick came up to her, his ice cream cone in his hand, and stood next to her under the lights in front of the ice cream store.

"Hey," she said, giving him a warm smile.

"We got him out, did you see it?" Nick asked her.

She nodded, her eyes twinkling. "It was awesome, wasn't it?"

"Unreal!" he agreed. "And, um, I wanted

to thank you. The slider was your idea, and . . . and it was a good one."

Morgan's eyes widened in surprise and pleasure. "Thanks!" she said. "You threw a great pitch."

"Thanks." He looked away, grateful that she'd chosen not to rub it in. "By the way—about our project?"

"Listen, Nick," she interrupted him. "I was thinking. It wasn't entirely your fault we got a C-minus."

"It wasn't?" he asked.

"No. Elliott and 'Slaw quit on us because we were both acting like idiots, arguing instead of working as a team."

"Right!" Nick said, agreeing with all his heart. The jersey had taught him that he had to work *with* his teammates, not lord over them. And now that he'd learned his lesson . . .

THE SWEET TASTE OF VICTORY

"I was thinking," said Nick, "we might be able to get our grade up if we handed in another poster, one we all worked on together."

Morgan considered it for a moment. "It might work," she said. "It's worth a try, anyway. Count me in. Hey, Elliott!" she called, as he came out of the store, holding a huge, dripping cone in his hand.

Coleman came out behind them, and two minutes later, the Monday Night Football Club had their group project all planned out.

They couldn't wait to see the look on Mr. Chambers's face!

"Hey, Mr. Chambers!" Morgan shouted.

Their history teacher turned around, and gave Morgan and the others a big smile. They were standing together in the hallway by the gym, holding between them the incredible poster they'd created the night before.

It was really three posters taped together at the sides to make one really long one—a triptych, Nick's dad had called it. Across the middle, in big, three-dimensional letters they'd all built together, were the words, "Got Freedom?" On the letters' faces were pasted the faces of kids from all over the world, cut out of magazines. To the right of "Got" was half of a globe, sticking out from the poster board, showing the Americas.

On the left of the poster was a pouch containing the group's research, with pictures of George Washington and other Revolutionary War leaders, and a little sign that said THE MEN AND THEIR FIGHT.

On the right was their essay, with a

picture of the Liberty Bell, and a little sign that said LIBERTY: WHAT'S A BELL TO YOU?

Mr. Chambers looked really impressed as he stared at them, standing there in the school hallway with kids rushing by in all directions. The poster was two days late, but it was better than nothing—and definitely better than Nick's pathetic solo effort.

"Check it out, Mr. Chambers!" Morgan said. "The slogan was Nick's idea," she added, making sure to give credit where credit was due.

"And making it three-dimensional was Morgan's idea," Elliott added, causing Morgan to blush with pride.

"And Elliott did most of the research," Nick piped up.

"They all thought it should include the whole world," Coleman said. "Er, I was just an observer," he added quickly.

They nodded at Mr. Chambers, to show that it was all true, they'd all done it together, with a little help from 'Slaw, of course.

Mr. Chambers beamed at them. "See what you can do when you work together?" he said, nodding at them approvingly.

"So . . ." Elliott said, "how about another look at the old grade book? Maybe rethink that C-minus?"

Morgan held her breath, waiting for Mr. Chambers's answer. "Absolutely!" he said, giving them another big smile.

The MNFC gang whooped it up, celebrating and high-fiving it, until Mr. Chambers cleared his throat, and added, "C-plus!"

Their smiles vanished, but only for a

moment. "Hey," Morgan said to the others, "it's an improvement."

"It's a whole grade improvement!" said Elliott. "Yes!"

"Yes!" Nick echoed, and soon, they were dancing around the hallway—a triumphant team celebrating yet another glorious victory.

They'd done it together, as team players.

FROM THE JERSEY #6
HEAD OVER HEELS

CHAPTER TWO

A BLOW FOR PERSONAL FREEDOM

"I can't believe this!" Elliott moaned. He paced back and forth in the Lighters' kitchen, while Morgan and Nick fixed snacks. It was seven o'clock, and the game would be starting any minute.

But Elliott wasn't through complaining. "I didn't know you can't skateboard in the park!" he protested, as if the policeman were still there. "I can't believe he took my board from me!"

"Take it easy, Elliott," Nick said.

"I've *got* to board," Elliott insisted. "I *live* to board!" He banged his fist down on the countertop. "Held down by 'the man' again!"

Morgan rolled her eyes. "You're getting your skateboard back in a month," she reminded him. "Relax!"

"Oh, yeah?" Elliott countered. "*You* try losing *your* identity for a month, and see how you like it."

The more Elliott thought about it, the angrier he got. Was it his fault if there was no good place to board in this stupid town? He'd been exercising his constitutional right to the pursuit of happiness, and the long arm of the law had reached out to stop him! It was not only unfair; it was downright unconstitutional!

"They may have taken my board," Elliott shouted, "but they can't take away my freedom!"

Morgan shook her head, smiling, and sighed. Nick carried the bowls of snack food into the den, then came back into the kitchen, carrying a football.

"Hey, where's Coleman?" he asked. "He's never been late for Monday Night Football." He passed the ball to Morgan, who caught it with one hand, without even looking.

"He didn't even call?" Morgan asked.

Nick picked up the kitchen phone, and dialed Coleman's number. But there was no answer, because at that moment, Coleman came through the Lighters' front door and waltzed into the kitchen.

Morgan heaved a huge sigh of relief, mingled with annoyance. "Hey, 'Slaw, where have you been?" she asked.

"Yeah," said Nick. "The game's already started." Inside the den, they could hear the roar of the crowd on TV as the Jets kicked off against the Cowboys.

Coleman took a step back. "Whoa," he said. "What's the big deal? I just had some homework to do."

Nick eyed him suspiciously. "'Slaw, it takes you five minutes to do your homework," he pointed out.

"Hey, I'm here now," 'Slaw said, sounding annoyed. "So let's just watch the game, okay?"

"Okay," Nick muttered.

"Okay," Morgan echoed softly.

"That's what I'm talking about," Coleman muttered, brushing past them and heading for the den. "Come on. Let's watch some Monday Night Football."

At halftime, they went back out into the kitchen to refill the snack bowls and put more ice in their glasses. Nick,

Morgan, and 'Slaw were all talking excitedly about the game.

But Elliott had barely been able to focus on football. He had no idea what the score was, and he didn't care. His mind was still on what had happened that afternoon. He couldn't get that policeman's angry glare out of his head.

What a travesty! The blatant injustice of it all! What did this town have against skateboarders anyway? Where were they supposed to express their artistry, if not at the park?

"I know!" he said out loud, snapping his fingers as the brilliant flash of an idea came to him. "We'll build our own half-pipe!" He clapped his hands in self-congratulation. "Yes! This is genius! No one can hold down a Rifkin!"